Emily
BUILDING
BRIDGES

JULIE LAWSON

EMILY
BUILDING
BRIDGES

JULIE LAWSON

PENGUIN
CANADA

PENGUIN CANADA

Penguin Group (Canada), a division of Pearson Penguin Canada Inc.,
10 Alcorn Avenue, Toronto, Ontario M4V 3B2

Penguin Group (U.K.), 80 Strand, London WC2R 0RL, England
Penguin Group (U.S.), 375 Hudson Street, New York, New York 10014, U.S.A.
Penguin Group (Australia) Inc., 250 Camberwell Road, Camberwell, Victoria 3124, Australia
Penguin Group (Ireland), 25 St. Stephen's Green, Dublin 2, Ireland
Penguin Books India (P) Ltd, 11, Community Centre, Panchsheel Park,
New Delhi – 110 017, India
Penguin Group (New Zealand), cnr Rosedale and Airborne Roads, Albany, Auckland 1310,
New Zealand
Penguin Books (South Africa) (Pty) Ltd, 24 Sturdee Avenue, Rosebank 2196, South Africa

Penguin Group, Registered Offices: 80 Strand, London WC2R 0RL, England

First published 2003

1 2 3 4 5 6 7 8 9 10   (WEB)

NATIONAL LIBRARY OF CANADA CATALOGUING IN PUBLICATION

Lawson, Julie, 1947–
Emily : building bridges / Julie Lawson.

(Our Canadian girl)
ISBN 0-14-301461-7

1. Chinese—British Columbia—Victoria—History—Juvenile fiction.
I. Title. II. Title: Building bridges. III. Series.

PS8573.A933E458   2003   jC813'.54   C2003-902890-9
PZ7

Visit the Penguin Group (Canada) website at **www.penguin.ca**

To the children of James Bay
Community School, Victoria, B.C.

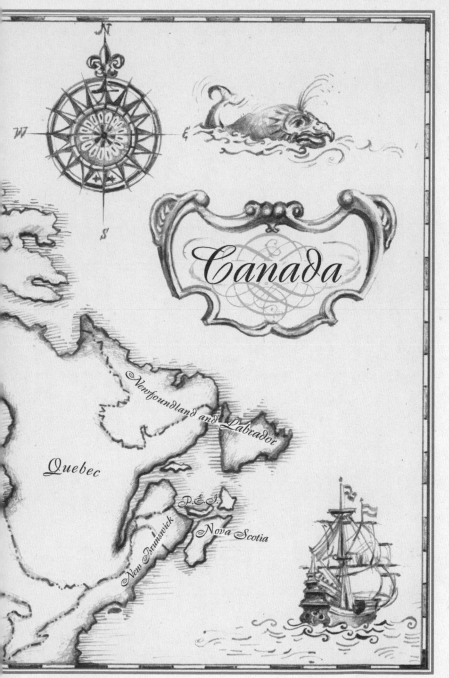

Canada

Newfoundland and Labrador

Quebec

P.E.I.

New Brunswick

Nova Scotia

 Marks the location of the story

EMILY'S STORY CONTINUES

AS 1897 IS USHERED IN, a celebration is in the works for the coming June, not only in Victoria but throughout the entire British Empire. The occasion will be Queen Victoria's Diamond Jubilee—sixty years on the throne!

In Victoria's Chinatown, the Chinese are celebrating the Year of the Rooster. In spite of the Head Tax introduced in 1885, the Chinese population has been steadily increasing. Chinatown is a vibrant community, with many retail stores, restaurants, two theatres, several temples, many gambling dens, and over ten opium factories. Opium manufacturing reaches its peak in the 1890s, to become one of Victoria's most valuable industries. It won't be banned until 1908.

There are very few Chinese women and children in Victoria, but the prospect of even a few children raises the question of their education. Children of wealthy merchants are often taught at home by private tutors, while other children attend local schools.

Anti-Oriental sentiments are still strong in British Columbia. Many white working men see the Chinese as a huge workforce, prepared to work for less money than their white counterparts. Signs such as "White Labour Only Employed" are not uncommon.

In this difficult climate, Hing's family arrives from China. Emily is excited by the prospect of meeting them. She is especially excited to finally meet Hing's daughter, Mei Yuk, and help her learn English.

And Emily has lessons of her own to look forward to. She and her sister Jane are about to take art lessons from a young woman named Emily Carr, who later in life becomes one of Canada's most famous painters.

But Emily is still haunted by memories of the 24th of May holiday when the Point Ellice Bridge collapsed and the streetcar she and her friends were riding on crashed into the waters of the Gorge. Will Emily be able to conquer her fears? And when her friendship with Hing's daughter sets her apart, will she have the courage to do the right thing?

CHAPTER N°. 1

Emily feels the ground give way, feels herself falling down with the bridge and the streetcar, down, down into the Gorge. Water rushes in, pulling her deeper. As she struggles, Alice grabs hold of her arm and won't let go.

Then she sees Florence floating by, pulling a girl by the hand—not up to the surface but down to the bottom. Florence smiles and says, "Look who I'm taking with me."

Emily looks and sees her own face staring back at her. The eyes are glazed with horror. The mouth is fixed in a scream . . .

Emily woke up sharply, the sound of the scream still ringing in her ears.

Within seconds, her mother was at her side, drawing her close. "There, there, Emily," she murmured. "It's all right."

"No, it's not." Emily choked back a sob. "Florence didn't move back to England. She drowned and I drowned and Alice . . ."

"No, dear. It's only a dream." Mother tucked her in and kissed her. "Go back to sleep. You'll get over your nightmares in time. You'll see."

But when? she wondered. And how?

When Emily awoke again in the morning, the questions were still on her mind. So too was the memory of the disaster that triggered the nightmares—the collapse of the bridge that sent an overcrowded streetcar, on which she and her friends were passengers, plunging into the waters of the Gorge.

It was now New Year's Day, 1897. Nearly eight months had passed since the disaster at Point Ellice Bridge, but the fear Emily had felt that day was still with her. During the summer, her nightmares had been so frequent and her cries so alarming that they'd consistently woken up the household. In the fall they had seemed to ease off, much to everyone's relief. But with the coming of winter and the approach of the new year, they were back again.

Emily thought she knew why. And, as the day progressed, she grew more and more anxious.

"Do we *have* to go to the Walshes' for dinner?" she kept asking. "Why can't we stay here?"

Try as she might, she could not convince her parents to change their plans. And that afternoon she found herself on a streetcar bound for the scene of the disaster.

Emily hadn't been near the Gorge since that terrible day. She'd almost gone in August, to her friend George Walsh's birthday party, but a stomach ache had kept her at home. The thought of going there now made her shudder.

Her younger sister Jane noticed her discomfort and patted her hand. "Don't be scared," she said.

"And don't worry," little Amelia said seriously.

"Your sisters are right," said Father. "It's a brand-new year. Let's put all our worries and fears behind us. What do you say?" He squeezed her shoulder as the streetcar drew up to the new Point Ellice Bridge and stopped to let them off. "Chin up! We'll cross each bridge as we come to it."

Emily dutifully stuck out her chin. At least she didn't have to cross *this* bridge—not today, anyway.

As the streetcar clanged its bell and went on its way, rolling onto the bridge, she turned quickly, refusing to look at the churning waters of the Gorge.

On the short walk to the Walshes' they passed another reminder of the tragedy—the home where Emily had been taken after her rescue. She hastened her step as the unwelcome memories began to flood in. The lawn, the bodies, the cries of anguish . . .

"Don't think about it," Mother said, as if reading Emily's mind. She gave her a reassuring hug.

It wasn't long before they reached the Walshes' house, where a large crowd had gathered to welcome in the new year.

George grabbed Emily's hand and tugged her away to his room. "Wait till you see my Christmas presents," he said.

"We want to see, too!" Jane followed, with Amelia at her heels.

He showed them his croquet set, complete with candle sockets attached to the wickets so they could play at night, and a new archery set.

"Are these arrows really—ouch!" cried Amelia.

"Yes, they're sharp!" Emily scolded. "You're not supposed to touch."

George laughed. "We can shoot arrows the next time you come."

"I'd rather play croquet," said Emily.

"I've got a new board game, too," said George. "Do you want to play?"

Soon all four were happily involved in a game of Snakes and Ladders.

As the afternoon wore on, and the guests were called to sit down for a festive dinner, Emily couldn't help but think back to the previous year, when the celebration had been at her house. That was when she'd first met George. What a trouble-maker he'd been then. To think that only a few months later, he would save her life!

During dinner there was the usual boring talk among the grown-ups, with a lot of big words Emily didn't understand. Last year she'd over-heard Father talking about an economic slump and tough times ahead. His words had proved to be true. Now he was saying that 1897 could mark a turnaround for the province.

The other guests agreed, voicing their opinions about the new parliament buildings, the booming mining industry in the interior, the construction of new railway lines . . .

Emily stifled a yawn.

Across the table, George was trying to make her and her sisters laugh, first by waggling his eyebrows, then by wiggling his ears. Jane looked back at him, cross-eyed. Amelia stuck out her tongue. Emily had to put her napkin to her mouth to hold in the giggles.

The end of the meal brought on the usual toasts, beginning, as always, with one to Queen Victoria. "The Queen!" Mr. Walsh said. "In the year of her Diamond Jubilee. Sixty glorious years on the throne."

Everyone stood up, raised his glass, and repeated, "The Queen! On her Diamond Jubilee!"

There was a buzz of excitement as they discussed the celebrations being planned to mark the occasion, not only in Victoria but throughout the entire British Empire.

"The 24th of May won't be nearly so grand this year," someone said. "All the stops are being pulled out for the Jubilee in June."

"From what I've heard," a newcomer to Victoria remarked, "the 24th of May wasn't so grand last year. Wasn't it just out here, on the Gorge—?"

"Don't!" Emily burst out without thinking.

A heavy silence fell over the room.

"Oh, dear," the man said. "I am sorry."

Mr. Walsh cleared his throat. "Another toast is in order. To the memory of those who lost their lives in the disaster. To those who mourn their loss. And to those who survived."

"And to Emily," George said earnestly. He raised his glass in her direction and the others followed suit.

Emily blushed to the tips of her ears. It was the first time she'd ever been toasted.

That night, as the girls were lying in bed, Amelia asked, "What's a *diamond julibee*? Is it like a necklace?"

"It's *jubilee*," Emily corrected. "And it's not jewellery, it's a celebration. Queen Victoria's been the Queen for sixty years, and that's why it's called 'diamond.' When she was Queen for fifty years, it was the Golden Jubilee."

"What happened at the *golden julibee*?"

"Amelia, it's *jubilee!* And I don't remember. I was only a year old."

"Queen Victoria's been the Queen for a long time," said Jane. "Even before Mother and Father were born."

"Listen, Em," Amelia piped up. "I know another *julibee*."

"Jubilee!"

"It's your birthday—on January 28. You'll be eleven. You'll be too old to have nightmares."

Emily could only hope that she was right.

CHAPTER N°·2

"Make a wish!" said Alice.

Emily looked at the shining candles on her cake and thought for a moment. She already had her bicycle. All she wanted now was an end to the nightmares. She made her wish and blew out the candles in one breath.

Amelia clapped her hands. "Happy *julibee,* Emily!"

Emily smiled. She no longer bothered to correct her sister. In fact, she was beginning to think that *julibee* should be a proper word, used for all manner of festive occasions.

It certainly described her birthday. She'd ridden to school that morning in a colourful whirl of red, pink, yellow, and blue, thanks to the ribbons her sisters had secretly tied onto the spokes of her bicycle wheels. Alice, her very best friend, had come for supper and given her a new bell for her bicycle. Jane and Amelia had drawn her a picture to hang on their bedroom wall. It showed Emily biking along the water-front, accompanied by leaping whales, a soaring eagle, and a flock of seagulls. Her parents had given her a box of watercolours and told her that, come April, she'd be taking art lessons along with Jane. This was a pleasant surprise for both girls! And Mother had made Emily's favourite dinner—roast beef with Yorkshire pudding and mashed potatoes, and birthday cake for dessert.

Emily was about to have a second helping of cake when she heard a knock at the back door.

"It's Hing!" she exclaimed. It was her first birthday without Hing, who had once been her family's cook, and she missed him. But Hing had finally been able to bring his family to Canada, and Emily was looking forward to meeting his daughter, Mei Yuk. Maybe Hing had brought Mei Yuk to surprise her!

"Manners, Emily!" Father called as she ran from the room. "It's not a race!"

Emily flung open the door and greeted Hing with a hug. He hadn't brought Mei Yuk, but at least he hadn't forgotten her birthday.

"Come in!" she said. "Do you want some of my birthday cake? It's a tipsy cake, with custard and almonds."

"No cake, please," Hing said. "No time. Restaurant very busy. But here. Happy birthday." He handed her a box of his tasty lemon tarts and a brightly decorated scroll. "For Chinese New Year. Next week, Year of Rooster. You and family come to Beautiful Jade Dragon Restaurant at noon for New Year banquet. I already speak to your father. It is all arranged."

"And then can I meet Mei Yuk?" Emily asked.

Hing smiled proudly. "You can meet whole Hing family!"

All week long Emily thought about Mei Yuk. What would she be like? She already knew that Hing's youngest child had been born in the Year of the Dog, the same year as she was. According to Hing, that meant that both girls could be selfish and stubborn. But they were also honest, loyal, and industrious—and champions of justice.

Emily pictured the two of them visiting the shops in Chinatown, sampling the New Year's treats and collecting the "lucky money" in *lai see* envelopes. Maybe they could even go to a Chinese opera together!

On the morning of the Chinese New Year, Emily ate a hurried breakfast, finished her chores, and set off on her bicycle. The rest of her family would be at Hing's restaurant at noon, but Emily just couldn't wait.

Chinatown was bursting with firecrackers when she arrived, and throngs of people were gathering to usher in the Year of the Rooster. At Hing's busy restaurant, every table was occupied. Emily looked around and saw two young waiters bustling among the customers, loaded down with platters of food. They paused when they saw her, exchanged a few words in Cantonese, and grinned broadly.

"You . . . Em-ry!" the younger one said. "Yes?"

"Yes," she replied. Then it dawned on her. "You must be Hing's sons."

"Hing, yes! Now . . . wait, please." The older one served his customers and disappeared behind a bamboo curtain. A short time later he returned with Hing.

"Em-ry, meet my sons!" Hing beamed. "Bak Cheun, number-one son. Gum Gin, number-two son. I told them to watch for a little girl with yellow hair, pink cheeks, and bicycle."

"Welcome to Victoria, British Columbia, Canada," Emily said. "I'm pleased to meet you. But where is Mei Yuk?"

At the mention of Mei Yuk, Hing and the boys looked at one another with grave expressions. "Sorry, Em-ry," Hing said. "Mei Yuk upstairs. Very shy. Afraid to come down."

"I could go upstairs and see her," Emily offered. "May I?"

Hing's face brightened. "This way," he said. "Stairs through kitchen."

Emily followed him into the kitchen, where a woman stood over the stove, frying bite-sized portions of meat and vegetables.

"My wife," Hing said proudly.

She looked up from her cooking and gave Emily a warm smile. *"Gung hey fat choy!"*

"Welcome to Victoria," Emily said. *"Gung hey fat choy!"*

Hing showed her the stairs, and she soon found herself in a small room above the kitchen. Adjoining it was another room with two windows and a door that opened onto a balcony. Both rooms were crammed with rough bits of furniture. A door laid out on two sawhorses formed a table, and an assortment of crates served as chairs. Elsewhere, Emily noticed a stack of faded quilts and a few pictures that she thought might be of Chinese gods. There was no sign of a person.

"Hello!" She waited, but there was no answer. She was about to leave when a faint rustling caught her attention. "Mei Yuk?"

A small girl dressed in red crept out from behind a carved wooden screen. She glanced at Emily from beneath her bangs, then lowered her head and stared fixedly at the floor.

It wasn't the reception Emily had been expecting.

"Gung hey fat choy," she said. "I'm Emily." Mei Yuk did not look up, but Emily pressed on. "I like your dress. It's red for good luck, isn't it? For Chinese New Year."

There was still no response. But why would

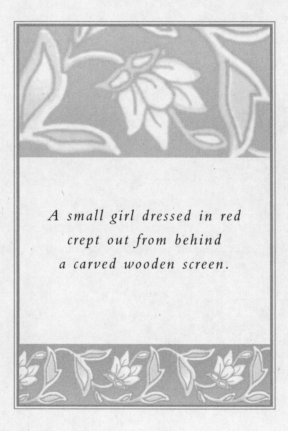

*A small girl dressed in red
crept out from behind
a carved wooden screen.*

there be? Emily chided herself. Mei Yuk didn't understand English.

She tried another approach. "Do you want to collect some *lai see* envelopes with me, and see the firecrackers?" She extended her hand, hoping that Mei Yuk would at least understand the gesture. But instead of accepting Emily's hand, Mei Yuk shook her head firmly and scurried back to her hiding place.

Crushed with disappointment and confused by Mei Yuk's reaction, Emily went back downstairs. What did I do wrong? she wondered. She'd sent Mei Yuk letters and lucky money and wanted to be her friend. So why didn't Mei Yuk like her?

As she entered the kitchen, Hing and his wife looked up hopefully. Their expressions faded, however, when they saw that she was alone.

"No Mei Yuk?" said Hing's wife.

"No," Emily said sadly.

Hing sighed. "Maybe after New Year, when everything is quiet. Come back then, see Mei Yuk."

Only if she wants to see me, Emily said to herself.

"But today, at noon, you come with family," Hing went on. "Special banquet for New Year." He gestured to the pieces of chicken spread out on the chopping block. "Chicken bring many good things in the new year. And make you run fast! Ready for next race."

Emily smiled, remembering the dishes that he'd cooked to prepare her for the Victoria schools' sports day: rice for energy, chicken for strength and speed. She hoped he could cook something special for Mei Yuk, something that might give her courage.

Since Mei Yuk wouldn't join her, Emily visited a few shops by herself, sampling the nuts and sweets offered by the merchants and collecting her own *lai see* envelopes. Then she stood outside Hing's and watched the long strings of firecrackers exploding in ear-splitting bursts and covering the ground with bits of red paper.

When Emily's family arrived at the restaurant,

Hing welcomed them and showed them to a special table.

"Did you meet Mei Yuk?" Mother asked, after they were seated.

Emily nodded. "But she hardly even looked at me. She made me feel like a bully."

"She hasn't been here very long," Father reminded her. "It's a big adjustment for her, for all of them, being in a new country. Especially when they can't speak the language."

"And don't forget," Mother added, "she scarcely knows her own father. He's like a stranger. When you think about it, Hing knows you better than he knows Mei Yuk."

"Maybe she's jealous," Jane remarked.

"She needn't be," said Emily. "I only want to be friends."

"Don't push too hard," Father said. "Give her time."

"Bother time," Emily muttered. Why did everything important have to take time?

CHAPTER № 3

A few days later, Emily and Alice were sprawled across Emily's bed, reading her mother's latest magazine from England. It had a special section for girls, with contests and activities as well as advice, some of which Emily tried to follow.

"Listen to this, Alice," she said. "'Are you helping someone else to have a good time? The root of perfect pleasure is unselfishness.'"

"I thought it was having a bicycle," Alice teased.

Emily ignored her and read on. "'The cheery, bright, everyday girl with no accomplishments to boast of—except for the great attraction of

22

thoughtfulness for others—is the one who can provide the oil that makes the wheel of life go round smoothly.' Goodness, what a confusing sentence."

"What does it mean?" Alice asked.

"It means you should be nice to people," Emily said. "Especially if you don't have any accomplishments."

"You've got accomplishments," Alice pointed out. "Is that why you weren't nice to Florence?"

"I *was* nice to Florence," Emily argued. "I saved her life, didn't I?"

"I meant before that."

"Alice, *she* wasn't nice to *me*. Not at first. She was always leaving me out of things. And then she made me trip so she could beat me in the school race." She paused. "I dream about her, you know. We're in the streetcar, you and me and Florence, and the water—"

"What's a wheel of life?" Alice abruptly changed the subject.

Emily sighed. She longed to talk to Alice about the disaster. After all, Alice had been on the streetcar with her, and she'd nearly drowned too. She was the only person Emily knew who could really understand what she'd been through. But Alice refused to discuss it. For her, it was as if the events of that day had never happened.

"A wheel of life?" Emily repeated. "I'm not sure, but it's given me an idea. Remember what I told you about Mei Yuk, and how scared she was when she saw me? Well, I'm going to be the oil that makes her life run smoothly."

Alice frowned. "What do you mean, you're going to be the oil?"

"Not *real* oil. It's like—what was that word we learned in composition? When you compare one thing with something else. Not a semaphore . . ."

"A metaphor!" Alice said. "Now I see. Can I help with Mei Yuk? Maybe we could have a party."

"Yes!" said Emily. "A Welcome to Victoria party!"

They warmed to the idea, but decided to wait a few weeks in order to give Mei Yuk more time to learn English.

"I'll go to Chinatown with you and help teach her," Alice said. "If Ma lets me."

"Let's go on Saturday," Emily suggested. "We'll teach her all the words she'll need to know for our party. Like *pin the tail on the donkey* and *blind-man's buff*."

"And *charades* and *raspberry cordial*."

"And we'll call our party . . ." Emily thought for a moment, then remembered what Mei Yuk's name meant in English. "We'll call it the Beautiful Jade Jubilee!"

"I'm not allowed to go," Alice grumbled the following day. Emily had stopped to get Alice on her way to school, and they were walking their bicycles together. "Ma says that Chinatown is a filthy den of iniquity, whatever that means. And it's full of unsavoury heathens who do nothing but gamble and smoke opium. And she's never even been there! It's a good thing she never found out about the time we went with George and Tom."

Emily agreed. Then she said, "Would it help if my mother spoke to your mother?"

Alice shook her head. "It's not only her. It's Pa, too. And once they make up their minds . . . Are you still going?"

"Of course," said Emily. "My mother doesn't mind, as long as I go straight to Hing's and come straight home. Hing thinks it might help Mei Yuk. Father told him to expect me on Saturday morning." She grinned. "It'll be like playing school, only I'll have a real pupil."

The pupil in question looked none too eager when Emily arrived on Saturday morning. She was in the kitchen washing dishes and did not even glance in Emily's direction. Nor did she stop working.

A stern word from her mother made her look up from her task. And, after Hing launched into a stream of Cantonese, she nodded reluctantly, dried her hands, and trudged upstairs.

"I tell her, speak English for two hours," Hing explained.

"Good," Emily said. "I can teach her a lot in two hours."

Upstairs, she was encouraged to find Mei Yuk sitting at the makeshift table instead of hiding behind the screen.

"I am sitting down," Emily said, joining her. "Can you say that?"

Mei Yuk gave her a blank look.

"I am sitting down." Emily repeated the words in a louder voice, but got another blank look— this time, with a hint of fear.

She lowered her voice and tried again. "You are sitting down."

Mei Yuk stared at her hands.

"I am standing up." Emily did so, but Mei Yuk didn't raise her eyes.

Exasperated, Emily pointed to herself, and then to Mei Yuk. "Me. You. Mei Yuk. Beautiful Jade. Can you say it in English? Me, Emily. You, Mei Yuk. Father, Hing. Can you say that? Hing. Father."

A tear rolled down Mei Yuk's cheek.

"Oh, no!" Emily wailed. "Please don't cry! I didn't mean to upset you." Taking out her handkerchief, she leaned across the table and wiped away the tear. "There," she said softly. She took consolation in one small victory—at least Mei Yuk hadn't flinched or run away.

What to do next? She'd made her pupil cry and hadn't taught her a single thing. She was hopeless as a teacher, and hopeless at making Mei Yuk's life run smoothly. But the two hours weren't over yet. There was time to try something else.

"I am sitting down," she said. "Now I am standing up. Sit down, stand up. A toast to Mei Yuk!" She raised an imaginary glass and saw Mei Yuk's eyes flicker. "You're watching now, aren't you? Well then, goodbye!" She walked behind the wooden screen, waited for a moment and returned to the table. "Hello, Mei Yuk. I'm Emily. I am sitting down." Then, "I am standing up. Goodbye!" She went through the motions again and again. Sit down, stand up. Hello, goodbye.

She was nothing if not stubborn—a true sign of someone born in the Year of the Dog. The trouble was, Mei Yuk had the same trait.

On what felt like the hundredth time, she caught Mei Yuk holding her hand to her mouth. Her eyes were shining.

"Are you laughing at me?" Emily said. "Well, good." She bowed with a theatrical flourish. "Thank you, thank you."

"Thank . . . you," Mei Yuk whispered.

"What's that?" Emily cupped a hand to her ear. "Did you say something? Did you say thank you?"

Mei Yuk covered her mouth again, but not before Emily saw her smile.

"You're welcome!" she said. "Thank you. You're welcome."

Now what? Suddenly, charades came to mind. She played the part of a clown, clutching her belly and shaking with laughter. "Laugh! Ho, ho! Can you say that, Mei Yuk? Laugh!" Next, she acted out "cry," with a sorrowful face and exaggerated sobs. "Boo, hoo! Cry!"

"Cly," Mei Yuk said shyly.

"Yes!" Emily whooped with delight. "Laugh, cry, hello, goodbye!"

Before long, Mei Yuk was chanting along with her, still timidly, but no longer covering her mouth or staring at the floor. And Emily didn't mind that Mei Yuk's pronunciation wasn't perfect, or that she mixed up the *l* and *r* sounds. *Her-ro* for *hello* was good enough for Emily.

When Hing appeared, Mei Yuk surprised him and Emily by saying, "Hello, Father. Thank you."

Hing's smile widened. "Em-ry good teacher!"

Emily warmed at his praise but felt somewhat guilty. In all that time she'd hardly taught Mei Yuk anything. She was facing a monumental task. How would she manage next week?

Well, as Father would say, she'd cross that bridge when she came to it. If only Alice were there to help. They could act out all sorts of words and situations. Mei Yuk seemed to enjoy the charades part. But Emily couldn't teach *everything* that way. She'd be worn out.

Emily said goodbye to Mei Yuk—for real this time—and made her way out through the kitchen. As she left the restaurant she was hit by a strong, boiled-potato smell, a sure sign that opium was being cooked in at least one of the many opium factories. She'd once asked her father why people smoked opium, and he'd told her that it gave them dreams. Emily couldn't understand it. She'd give anything *not* to have dreams.

She wondered about Mei Yuk's dreams. Did she dream about China? Did she have nightmares about being in a new country? Did she miss her friends? There was so much Emily wanted to know.

It suddenly occurred to her that she'd hardly ever seen children in Chinatown. No wonder Mei Yuk seemed sad. She had no one to play with.

Right then and there, Emily came up with a new plan. An even better plan, because next time Alice would be able to help. And, best of all, it would give Mei Yuk a chance to have some fun.

CHAPTER N⁰ 4

The following Saturday, Mei Yuk came to Emily's house. Everything had been arranged. Her brother Bak Cheun brought her and promised to fetch her in two hours' time.

After Emily had introduced Mei Yuk to her family, the girls set off for Alice's house. Emily chatted and pointed out various things along the way, hoping that Mei Yuk might remember at least a few new words.

"That's a house," she said. "And a tree . . ." *House, tree, streetcar, buggy, horse, bird* . . . so many words! "See the sun, Mei Yuk? It's sunny."

"Sun," Mei Yuk echoed. "Sunny."

"Good!" Emily smiled. "It's mild today, too. It's almost the end of February and it feels like spring. Look, there's an eagle! And seagulls!" She drew Mei Yuk's attention to a bald eagle being mobbed by a swarm of seagulls.

Mei Yuk gave her a worried look.

"It's all right," Emily said. "They can't hurt the eagle. He's too big. But they pester him something fierce, the bullies."

A moment later, the eagle landed at the top of a fir tree and added its screeching cry to that of the gulls. Mei Yuk pointed excitedly. "Eagle? Tree?"

"Yes, Mei Yuk! You're learning fast. Now, see that house with the blue trim? That's Alice's house."

They had no sooner stepped into the yard than Tom and George appeared. Tom took one look at Mei Yuk and sneered. "Who's that?"

"Mei Yuk," said Emily. "Hing's daughter."

"What are you doing with her?"

"I'm playing with her and teaching her English."

"So what's she doing here? You can't take her inside our house."

"I wouldn't want to!" Emily flared up angrily. "Anyway, I'm only coming to get Alice. We're going to the park."

"Not with Alice. Ma won't let her go with a—"

"Be quiet!" Emily snapped. The thought that Tom might spoil things, just when Mei Yuk was beginning to open up, was enough to get her blood boiling.

"Come on, Tom," George said. He gave Emily an apologetic shrug and pulled Tom away. "Let's bike over to my place."

"You're wasting your time," Tom flung over his shoulder. "Alice won't go near one of those heathens."

"You don't even know what a heathen is!" Emily was determined to have the last word.

At that moment, Alice called out from an upstairs window, "Go on without me, Em. I'll meet you at the hill."

Her words made Emily wonder if Tom had been right. But she walked on with Mei Yuk and tried not to worry.

They had just reached the hill when Alice came running up. "Sorry," she said. "I had to help Ma with the dusting."

Emily smiled with relief. "So you were allowed to come?"

"Of course! Why not?"

"Well, Tom said . . ."

"Oh, bosh! Don't listen to what he says." She turned her attention to Mei Yuk. "Hello, Mei Yuk. I'm Alice Kerr."

Mei Yuk smiled shyly. "Hello," she said.

"Let's go up the hill," said Emily. "See, Mei Yuk?" She pointed to the summit. "Hill. Beacon Hill."

"Beacon Hill!" Mei Yuk grinned.

Suddenly they heard a high-spirited voice cry out, "Make way below!"

The girls looked up and gaped. "It's a lady!" Emily shrieked. "She's rolling down the hill!"

Rolling down Beacon Hill was a favourite pastime, but it was something that children did, not grown-up ladies. This lady might have been as old as *thirty!* They could even see her petticoat!

A black retriever bounded after her, barking excitedly.

By now the lady had stopped rolling and was getting to her feet, brushing bits of dirt and grass off her long, dark skirt. She saw the girls staring but didn't seem the least bit embarrassed. "What fun!" she said. "I've been wanting to do that for ages."

The dog woofed as if in agreement and cast a hopeful look to the top of the hill.

"Not now, Watch," the lady said, giving him a pat. "We'll come back another day." She smoothed her skirt and tucked a few loose strands of dark, curly hair into place. "Best thing for your health," she said, her eyes sparkling. "A good roll down a hill."

Still amazed, the girls watched her stride away. "Who is she?" Alice wondered.

"I don't know," said Emily. "But imagine, being grown-up and rolling down a hill."

"Wait till I tell Ma." Alice giggled. "She'll say it's scandalous."

"And it is!" Emily yelped. "Let's do it, too!"

And they all three went rolling down Beacon Hill.

After feeding the ducks, the girls strolled back to Alice's house, where she invited them in for a cup of cocoa. They were sitting at the kitchen table enjoying themselves when Mrs. Kerr walked in.

"A word, Alice, if you please," she said curtly.

Alice excused herself and followed her mother into the hall.

Emily couldn't help but overhear their conversation. She grew hot with a mixture of anger and shame. Thank goodness Mei Yuk couldn't understand.

"I won't have her in the house," Mrs. Kerr was saying. "Whatever were you thinking? She'll have to leave."

"But she's Emily's friend," Alice protested. "And my friend, too. We're teaching her English."

"Might as well teach a goose," her mother snorted. "I won't have it, Alice. If your father finds out . . . And as for the cup she's using, you be sure to wash it twice, in scalding water. She's probably contagious. Chinatown is a filthy, disease-ridden—"

"But Emily—"

"That's another thing. As long as Emily . . ." She lowered her voice.

Emily couldn't bear to hear any more. Seeing that Mei Yuk had finished her cocoa, she took the two cups and placed them side by side on the counter. Let Mrs. Kerr figure out which was which.

"Goodbye, Alice," she called out. "Thank you for the cocoa."

"Thank you," Mei Yuk said in her turn. "Goodbye."

Some goose! Emily smiled with pride.

It took more than Mrs. Kerr's words to discourage Emily from her goal. Every Saturday morning Bak Cheun would bring Mei Yuk to Emily's house to learn English. If it wasn't raining, the girls went to the park or to the beach. Otherwise, they stayed indoors. Alice sometimes met them on their outings or joined them at Emily's, but there were no more invitations to her house.

When Emily told Alice that she'd overheard her mother's remarks, Alice flushed with embarrassment and said she was sorry.

"As long as you don't feel the same way," Emily said. "You don't, do you?"

After a slight hesitation, Alice said, "No . . ."

It wasn't quite the wholehearted assurance Emily had been expecting.

For a while, Emily hoped that the time she was spending with Mei Yuk would put the Point Ellice Bridge disaster out of her mind and bring an end to her nightmares. But they continued.

One Saturday, after Emily had had a particularly bad night, Mei Yuk asked if she was feeling all right.

"I'm tired," Emily admitted. "I keep having nightmares."

"What is *nightmare*?" Mei Yuk asked.

"I'll show you." Emily pretended to fall asleep, waited a moment and woke up with a loud scream. "That's a nightmare," she said. "A very bad dream."

Mei Yuk nodded gravely. "Me, too. Nightmare. Very many people. Father, Mother, brother, nowhere. I cry many tear. I . . . found?"

"I think you mean lost," Emily said. She gave Mei Yuk's hand a sympathetic squeeze.

The next day, when Emily got home from Sunday School, Hing and Mei Yuk were waiting. They handed her two identical pictures showing a Chinese warrior from ancient times. He had a ferocious scowl, a dagger at his waist, and several gruesome objects hanging from his belt, including a skull.

"For nightmare," Mei Yuk explained.

Emily was puzzled. It was the sort of picture that might cause *more* nightmares.

"There's a story," Hing said. He told her about a Chinese emperor who had once had a terrible time with nightmares. Night after night he'd woken up screaming. Finally he'd ordered two of his fiercest warriors to stand guard outside his bedroom door and scare away the nightmares. His plan worked, and he was able to sleep.

But the warriors grew weary. All night long they stood on guard. All day long they fought in battles. They finally decided to hang pictures of themselves outside the Emperor's door instead, so that they could get some sleep.

"Now called Door Guardians," Hing said, pointing to the pictures. "As good as real warriors. Scare away your nightmares."

That night, Emily tacked the pictures on either side of her bedroom door, hoping she'd have a peaceful sleep. But again she woke up in the dark, her heart racing, another vision of deep water and a feeling of helplessness fading slowly from her mind.

The Door Guardians might have worked for that emperor, she thought, but they are certainly not helping me.

On the first Saturday in April, Alice showed up at Emily's. Two weeks had gone by since she'd last seen Mei Yuk, and she was surprised by her progress.

"Father talk English," Mei Yuk said. "Em-ry good teacher. Monday, school."

"I know," Alice groaned. "I hate Mondays."

"It's not that, Alice," Emily said excitedly. "She means that she's going to school on Monday."

"What? Where?"

"South Park! She's going to be in our class. It's all arranged."

"Why *our* school?"

"Because she knows me and I can help her, and it's not that far for her to come. Maybe in a couple of weeks we can finally have our party. Remember, the Beautiful Jade Jubilee?" Something in Alice's expression made her pause. "You still want to, don't you?"

"Yes, but . . ."

"Charade!" Mei Yuk broke in. "Can we play?"

Emily readily agreed, relieved that Mei Yuk had changed the subject.

They played until it was time for Alice to go home for dinner. She and Emily were on the porch, saying goodbye, when they saw Tom walking down the street. Alice quickly stepped back inside the house.

"What's the matter?" Emily asked.

"Nothing . . ."

Emily had an inkling. "You're not allowed to come over, are you? As long as I'm seeing Mei Yuk. Your mother—"

"It's not just Ma." Alice looked away, clearly uncomfortable. "Pa belongs to some group that doesn't like the Chinese."

"Well . . . what if he finds out you're coming here anyway?"

"I'll probably get a licking."

"What?" Emily was shocked. She knew that Alice's father had a temper, but to punish Alice for something like *that*? "Then you can't come." She spoke without hesitation. She wouldn't be

responsible for her best friend getting in trouble at home. "You'll just have to wait until Mei Yuk's not here."

"I could come back after dinner," Alice said. "Mei Yuk goes home at noon, doesn't she?"

"Yes, but my art lessons start this afternoon. Jane and I are going together. Didn't I tell you?"

"No." Alice looked hurt. "You don't tell me anything any more."

"Oh, Alice. Don't feel badly. Mei Yuk's lessons won't go on forever. She's such a fast learner, and once she starts school she won't need extra lessons from me. Pretty soon we can spend every Saturday morning together, just like before."

"Promise?"

"Of course. You're my best friend, remember? Nothing can change that."

CHAPTER N°6

"I hope Miss Carr won't think I'm too hopeless," Emily said as she and Jane set off for their art class. She was excited, but a little apprehensive. After all, their teacher wasn't just a teacher. She was a real artist. She'd studied art in San Francisco. She'd even won first prize for a drawing at the Victoria Fall Fair.

Miss Carr lived close to Beacon Hill Park, so it wasn't long before they were knocking on her door.

A stern-looking woman appeared. "If you're here for my sister's art lessons," she said, "they're in the old cow barn."

"The barn?" The girls raised their eyebrows.

"Out the back," she said, and closed the door.

"Does 'old cow barn' mean an old cow or an old barn?" Jane wondered as they walked around to the back.

"I don't know," said Emily. "But there's an old barn. And listen."

The sound of children's voices and laughter drifted down from high up in the barn.

"That's George!" Emily said, recognizing his familiar laugh. "I hope he behaves."

"The lessons must be in the hayloft," Jane remarked. "We'll have to go up the stairs."

A newly built wooden staircase led up the outer wall of the barn to a wide double door in the loft. The girls had almost reached the top of the stairs when a dog burst out onto the landing, followed by a pleasant-looking woman.

"Hello, girls," she said. "You must be Jane and Emily."

Emily took one look at the round, rosy face

and dark, curly hair and blurted out, "You're the lady I saw rolling down the hill!" Goodness! And she was their teacher?

"Quite right," the woman laughed. "I'm Miss Carr. A dedicated roly-poly. And I'm an Emily too, like you."

Emily beamed.

"Come in and join the others, Jane and Emily Too. Sit wherever you like. It's not raining so there's no need to worry about the skylight leaking. And don't mind the dog. Watch loves company."

Watch gave a friendly woof and wagged his tail.

There were six pupils, including George, and everyone was given a sketch pad, a pencil, and a stick of charcoal.

"Use your pencils and draw what you see," Miss Carr said, indicating the various objects she'd placed on the table. An apple. A plaster hand. A plaster foot. A stuffed raven. Emily drew the objects as faithfully as she could, but took time to observe her surroundings.

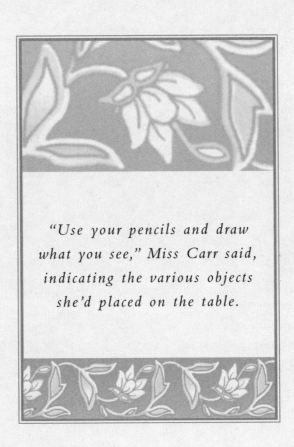

"Use your pencils and draw
what you see," Miss Carr said,
indicating the various objects
she'd placed on the table.

The converted loft, high in the middle and low at the sides, was rustic with its knotholed floor and burlap-covered walls. A big coal-oil lamp hung from a rafter, so Miss Carr could work at night, Emily supposed. Her teacher's paints and brushes, sketches and canvases were spread across a smaller table or stacked against the walls.

It was cozy in the studio, bright and warm with a fire crackling in the woodstove. The smells of hay and apples and new-sawn wood rose from below, and Emily could hear a cow chewing and the clucking of chickens. There was also the chatter and laughter of Miss Carr and her pupils. It wasn't a bit like school. Miss Carr even surprised them once and a while by singing out loud!

Every so often the shrill cry of a peacock filled the room, followed by a series of angry yaps from Watch. The first time this happened, Miss Carr explained that the peacock had come from Beacon Hill Park and was making his daytime quarters on the studio roof. "He likes to strut before the dormer window," she said. "He uses it as a mirror! And he loves to get a rise out of Watch. Silly old dog. You'd think he'd know by now."

After finishing his sketch of the raven, George asked, "Can we draw Watch?"

"I'd have to stuff him first," Miss Carr replied. She laughed as her pupils gasped with horror. "You sillies! You know I'd never do such a thing. And of course you may draw him. Watch loves to pose."

At the end of the first hour, Miss Carr left the studio and returned a few minutes later with a basket of fresh bread. "One slice is all you need for now," she said.

Only one slice? Emily swallowed her disappointment. At least they were thick slices. Would there be butter, too? Devonshire cream? Strawberry preserves? She grinned at Jane across the table. Mother hadn't mentioned that their art lessons would include snacks.

"Now tear it into chunks," said Miss Carr.

Emily frowned but followed the instructions. Then she sampled a piece. It tasted as good as it smelled.

"We're going to draw with charcoal," Miss Carr explained. "Charcoal will free things up, give you the lights and the darks. Study the forms and practise the shapes. If you need to erase anything, use the bread."

"The bread?" Emily was aghast.

"Did you think it was for tea?" Miss Carr said. "No, the bread's for rubbing out."

"Can't we have a little bite?" George asked.

"No, sir! Not even a nibble."

The studio was soon littered with charcoal-blackened crumbs and crusts. More bread was sliced and torn into chunks. "It's not for eating!" Miss Carr kept reminding them, but no one could resist.

Before Emily knew it, the class was over.

"Time for tea," Miss Carr announced as the kettle on the woodstove began to whistle. "Emily Too, you can pass the cookies."

After tea, Miss Carr collected everyone's class fees and put the coins into a boot. Then she hung the boot from a rafter by the door. "Next week," she said, "just pop the money into the boot when you arrive."

"What will you do with it all?" Jane asked.

Miss Carr smiled. "As soon as the boot's full, I'm going to London to study art."

"But you're already an artist," said Emily.

"Not yet!" she said. "I've got so much to learn."

"I don't understand," Jane said as they were walking home. "Being as old as Miss Carr and still wanting to learn things. I thought that when you grew up you knew everything."

"She doesn't act old," Emily remarked. "Not like a teacher. You should have seen her on the hill."

"She acts like one of us," said Jane. "I hope she never gets enough money to go away."

"Me too," said Emily. "I want to grow up and be just like her. And have a loft and invite my friends for tea. But I'll never be an artist."

"You might be," Jane said kindly.

"No, I don't think so. My raven looked more like a peacock. I'm hopeless! But it's such fun, I don't even care."

"I wish school were as much fun," said Jane.

Her words reminded Emily that Mei Yuk was starting school on Monday. What would it be like for her? Was she excited? She was bound to feel nervous, as Emily herself had felt on the way to art class. But hopefully, by the end of the day, things would turn out as well for Mei Yuk as they had for her.

Early Monday morning, Mei Yuk arrived at Emily's house ready for school. Her shoes were polished, her hands and face were scrubbed, her hair was shining, and she wore a crisp white pinafore. She smiled bravely at Bak Cheun as she said goodbye and clasped Emily's hand for the walk to school.

When they reached the school grounds, Alice called them over to join her and a group of friends. "This is Mei Yuk," she said. "She's going to be in our class."

The other girls exchanged glances. Some

smiled politely and said hello. A few walked away. Emily could hear them whispering and snickering behind her back. She could also hear the rude comments that some of the older boys were making, including Tom.

Mei Yuk noticed too. Although she couldn't understand what the boys were saying, there was no mistaking their tone. She stared at the ground and held Emily's hand more tightly.

It wasn't long before the principal, Miss Cameron, rang the bell and everyone went into the Assembly Hall for the morning exercises. Mei Yuk followed Emily's every move—standing for the singing of "O Canada" and "God Save the Queen," listening to the Bible reading, bowing her head for the saying of the Lord's Prayer.

After the assembly, the pupils filed off to their classrooms. Emily tried to ignore the looks cast in her and Mei Yuk's direction. Some were merely curious, but others were unfriendly, even hostile.

When they got to their classroom, Emily's teacher, Miss Wilson, greeted Mei Yuk warmly.

She gave her a slate and a chalk pencil and indicated to her that she could sit with Emily.

"I don't know how much you're able to understand," she said, "but your father has spoken to our principal and she has agreed to let you attend our class for a while, with other pupils your age, to see how you make out. I'm sure Emily will look after you."

Mei Yuk gave a small smile at the mention of Emily's name. As long as Emily was close by, she seemed to say, things would be fine.

The first hour passed quickly. Mei Yuk may not have understood much English, but she certainly understood numbers. She flew through the arithmetic questions that Miss Wilson put on the blackboard and ended up with more correct answers than many of her classmates.

When it was time for reading, Miss Wilson handed her an illustrated primer, the kind of book used by beginners.

"She should be in the primary school with the babies," one of the boys whispered. "She doesn't even know how to read."

Miss Wilson overheard. "I suppose you plunged straight into the third reader when you started school?"

"No, Miss," he replied.

"And since when have I allowed unkind remarks to be uttered in this classroom?"

"Never, Miss."

"Well, then? What do you have to say?"

"Sorry, Miss." But as soon as her back was turned, he looked over at Emily and glared.

Emily glared back. It wasn't *her* fault he had a big mouth.

Several of her classmates were still gawking, but Mei Yuk no longer seemed to notice. She held the primer as if she were handling a rare treasure. Then she placed it on the desk and gently ran her fingers over the cover.

"Open, close," Emily whispered, demonstrating with her reader.

Mei Yuk grinned. When she opened the primer and saw the first illustration, she gave an

audible gasp of pleasure. "Bird," she said, pointing. "Tree."

"Very good," said Miss Wilson. "Emily has
taught you well."

At recess, Emily and Mei Yuk once again found
themselves the centre of unwanted attention.
Several boys and girls were pulling faces and
calling them names.

"Just ignore them," said Alice. "Do you want to
play hopscotch?"

They showed her how to play and were happily
involved in the game when Tom swaggered over.

"You'd better clear off, Alice," he said.
"Remember what Ma said."

Alice threw her pebble and hopped onto the
squares without replying.

"I'll tell Ma," Tom persisted. "You'll get it when Pa comes home."

"Go away," said Emily. "She's not listening to you."

After taking her turn, however, Alice made an excuse and left to join her other friends.

Emily put on a brave face and tried not to care. Things would get better. Like Father always said, it was only a matter of time.

CHAPTER N.º 8

"You'd love my art class, Alice."

Three weeks had gone by. Alice had been away for most of it, stuck at home with a bad cold, and Emily had missed her. But now she was back at school. It was recess, and with Mei Yuk inside practising her printing, Emily and Alice were strolling about the playground arm in arm.

"It's such fun!" Emily continued. "Miss Carr sings out of tune and makes everyone laugh. There's a dog called Watch—remember, we saw him on the hill? And at the end of every class we have tea and cookies." She told Alice how shocked she'd been when she recognized Miss Carr, and how surprised she'd been to find out that George was taking lessons too.

"I heard about George," Alice remarked. "Tom won't have anything to do with him any more. He says he's a sissy, drawing and painting with girls."

"Well, it doesn't bother George. Wouldn't you like to take lessons? It might not be too late."

"I'd never be allowed," Alice said. "Ma knows all about Miss Carr. She says she's very odd. She goes on camping trips in the wilderness all by herself. And one day, Ma saw her out horseback riding—"

"What's wrong with that?"

"She wasn't riding sidesaddle, she was sitting astride, like a man! In long skirts! It's as bad as rolling down a hill. And a friend of Ma's saw her at a dance and said she just sat on the stairs and glowered. She's also bad-tempered—"

"She is not!"

"And she wears dowdy clothes and has no manners."

"That's not true!" Emily said hotly. "You shouldn't listen to gossip, Alice. Just because Miss Carr doesn't act like everybody else doesn't mean she's odd."

"Maybe you're right. Maybe it's *you* who's odd. You and that sissy, George."

"Oh, Alice!" Emily gave her a playful nudge, trying to lighten the mood. "Let's play the favourite game. You start."

"All right," said Alice. "And I'll be you. Favourite day? Saturday, because I won't have time to see Alice. I'll be too busy playing school with Mei Yuk in the morning and drawing with George in the afternoon."

"Alice—"

"Favourite subject? Art. Favourite pastime? Teaching Mei Yuk. Best friend? Mei Yuk."

"Alice, stop it! You know you're my best friend."

Alice let out a loud sigh. "I know. I'm just teasing. But honestly, Em, I never see you any more."

"Because you've been ill!"

"But before that." Alice pouted. "You're taking art lessons and spending all your spare time with Mei Yuk. It's just like the saying. Two's company, three's a crowd."

"You didn't think so last year when Florence was here," Emily reminded her. "Now you know how *I* felt."

"Yes, but that was different. Florence wasn't from China."

Emily groaned with frustration and switched to another topic. "Let's talk about the party. It's going to be this Friday. That is, if you're still coming."

"Of course!" Alice brightened. "I wouldn't miss a party, especially not a Jubilee."

By four o'clock on Friday afternoon, Emily had to face the fact that no one was coming to the

Beautiful Jade Jubilee. She had invited six girls from her class and all six had accepted. But no one had come. Not even Alice.

It was lucky that the party was supposed to be a surprise for Mei Yuk. She'd never have to know and be disappointed. Emily and her sisters taught her how to play pin the tail on the donkey and blindman's buff. Afterwards, they ate jam tarts and sipped raspberry cordial.

While they were waiting for Bak Cheun to fetch Mei Yuk, Emily showed her the drawings she'd done in her art class. To Emily's surprise, Mei Yuk admired them and asked if she might try.

"Sure," Emily said. She gave Mei Yuk some paper and charcoal, expecting her to copy some of Emily's sketches. Instead, Mei Yuk drew a river, some mountains, and a cluster of small huts.

"Home," Mei Yuk said. "China." With a few deft strokes she added chickens, dogs, water buffalo, and people.

Emily was impressed. "That's a beautiful picture," she said. "You can draw way better than

I can." She watched as Mei Yuk added more details to the scene, then asked, "Do you miss your home in China?"

"Miss?" Mei Yuk looked puzzled.

"Do you still feel lost?" Emily tried to explain. "Like in your nightmare?"

"No nightmare." Mei Yuk smiled. "Nightmare lost. You lost nightmare?" She gave Emily a hopeful look.

"Yes," Emily said. "The Door Guardians scared them away." It wasn't true, but she didn't want to hurt Mei Yuk's feelings.

When Bak Cheun arrived, Mei Yuk showed him her drawing, as well as the copybook Miss Wilson had given her. Mei Yuk knew her alphabet now, so she could practise printing words and simple sentences.

"Thank you, Em-ry," she said as she was leaving. "I am happy."

Emily smiled, warmed by the notion that she might have done a good job of oiling Mei Yuk's "wheel of life," at least for today. Maybe her mother's magazine was right, unselfishness *was* the root of perfect pleasure.

She was basking in the warm feeling when Alice unexpectedly came to the door.

"I'm sorry, Em," she said. There was a catch in her voice, and her eyes were red and swollen. "I can't come in. Ma told the other mothers that Mei Yuk was coming to the party. I didn't tell her. Tom did. And Ma told everyone that Mei Yuk was dirty and ill-mannered, and they're all signing a petition to ask the School Board to put her in a separate school because she has a bad influence on white children." She sniffed loudly and swallowed back a sob. "But that's not the worst of it."

Emily's stomach churned. Somehow she knew what was coming.

"Ma said that I'm not allowed to play with you, as long as you're friends with Mei Yuk. That you're becoming a bad influence, too. And not just because of Mei Yuk. It's also because of Miss Carr."

Emily was speechless. It was unfair, untrue, unkind, every "un" word she could think of. What was Alice asking of her? To choose between one friend and another? To give up her art lessons because of what some people thought about her teacher?

It wasn't so long ago that she'd wanted Alice to choose between her and Florence. Alice hadn't chosen; she'd wanted them all to be friends. Eventually the girls had worked things out themselves. But now, with parents involved, Emily would be forced to make a decision.

She swallowed hard. "I don't know what to say."

There was an awkward silence. Then they both spoke at once.

"Well . . ."

"I guess . . ."

"You first," said Alice.

"Well," Emily said, "I guess we'd better say goodbye."

Alice looked taken aback. "You mean you're not—?"

"No." Emily knew what Alice was expecting her to do. But she couldn't, not even for her best friend.

"Goodbye, then," Alice said sadly. She gave Emily a quick hug, then turned and walked away.

Unable to hold back the tears, Emily ran to her room and flung herself across the bed.

Her mother came in after her. "Emily, what is it?"

"Alice can't play with me any more," she sobbed. "Her mother—"

"Oh, dear. I know. Mrs. Kerr asked me to sign the petition too. Of course, I refused. I told her that Mei Yuk is a charming girl, clean, tidy, and diligent. I also told her that you're free to make your own decisions where friends are concerned, and that you're learning as much from Mei Yuk as Mei Yuk is learning from you."

This was a surprise. "What am I learning from her?" Emily asked. "I can't even speak her language."

"You're learning valuable lessons in becoming a good citizen," Mother said. "You're growing up strong and noble and true to yourself."

"I don't want to be all that! I just want Alice to like me again."

"She still likes you," Mother said. She drew Emily close and stroked her hair. "Don't worry. Things will work out in time, you'll see."

"Nothing works out in time," Emily argued. "You said my nightmares would end with time and they didn't. They're getting worse."

"That's because the 24th of May is coming up," Mother said. "It's on everyone's mind, the anniversary of the disaster. But once that's over ..." She gave Emily a hug. "I'm so proud of you. There isn't a single day that I don't thank God for your being here."

"But what should I do?" Emily said. "If Alice won't talk to me because of Mei Yuk—?"

"You'll know what to do. And remember, it's not what Alice wants, either. She's obeying her parents. As she should."

"Even when they're wrong?"

"Oh, Emily. That's one of the many things you learn when you're growing up. That, right or wrong, there are no easy answers."

"Where's Mei Yuk? She's always on time." Emily had been waiting anxiously for over twenty minutes for Mei Yuk to arrive so they could walk to school together. Was her friend ill? Was Bak Cheun unable to bring her? What if Mei Yuk had tried to come on her own and had got lost?

Another possibility came to mind. What if the School Board had accepted Mrs. Kerr's petition and told Mei Yuk she could no longer attend school?

"It's not that," Mother said. "I've learned that the School Board doesn't have the right to separate Chinese children from other children. And there's another thing you should know. Last week the Board asked the teachers for their opinion, and they praised Mei Yuk for her good behaviour and attitude."

"So where is she?" Emily continued to fret.

After another ten minutes had gone by, Mother said, "If you don't go now, you'll be late for school. You'll just have to leave without her."

Emily reluctantly agreed. But as she was setting off on her bicycle she thought, Why not go and look for Mei Yuk? I could bike at least as far as the James Bay Bridge and see if they're coming across. I'd still be on time for school.

When she reached the bridge, she stopped and looked. But there was no sign of Mei Yuk or her brother.

Something was wrong. Emily felt it in the pit of her stomach. There was only one thing to do—forget about school and keep going.

She was halfway across the bridge when she noticed a commotion on the beach. The tide was out, and the usual scavengers were on the mud flats, rummaging through cast-off boots, cooking pots, kettles, and the like. But the commotion was not coming from them. On the far shore, near the soap-works factory, a group of boys was chasing someone, yelling and throwing stones. Emily's heart clenched as she recognized Bak Cheun and, a little farther along, Mei Yuk.

A feeling of rage erupted inside. She pedalled furiously across the bridge and down the street. Then she dropped her bicycle at the factory and ran onto the shore.

By now, one of the boys had caught hold of Bak Cheun's pigtail and was laughing as Bak Cheun tried to fight him off. Mei Yuk had slipped and fallen in the mud, and the rest of the boys were swarming around her.

"You bullies!" Emily shrieked. "Leave them alone!"

The boys turned and glared. Tom was among them. He had Mei Yuk's copybook in his hand.

With a sneer at Emily, he hurled it into the factory sludge that spewed into the bay.

Emily glared back at the boys, her heart pounding. She was terrified that they might now turn on her. What could she do against five big boys? What could she say? "Leave Mei Yuk and her brother alone or I'll tell your parents"? Tom's parents wouldn't care. They didn't go as far as throwing stones, but their words and actions were every bit as hurtful.

Just then, one of the scavengers looked up from his rummaging. Seeing what was going on, he straightened up and came towards the boys. "Clear off, lads," he said gruffly. "You've had your fun."

His words prompted Emily into action. She pushed past the boys and helped Mei Yuk to her feet. Then she retrieved the copybook and wiped it off as best she could.

Tom and the others laughed unpleasantly as they swaggered off.

"You're a bunch of seagulls!" Emily hurled after them. "You think you're brave when you're in a

She pushed past the boys and helped Mei Yuk to her feet.

big mob." Turning to Mei Yuk, she said, "We can go to my house and get you cleaned up. You can wear one of my pinafores, and I've an extra pair of shoes. Don't worry about being late. Mother will write a note and explain everything."

"No," said Mei Yuk, reaching for her brother's hand. Her eyes welled up with tears.

Emily tried to reassure her. "It'll be better tomorrow. They won't bother you again."

"No," Mei Yuk repeated. "No school tomorrow. No school today. We go home now."

"But you can't!" Emily pleaded. "That's what they want."

Bak Cheun gave her a sombre look. "Every day is the same."

"What do you mean?"

"Same boy, other boy, always the same. Today, very bad."

"This happens every day?" A sob rose up in Emily's throat.

But how could she not have known? Memories of little things came flooding in. A torn page in

Mei Yuk's copybook, a bruise on her cheek . . .
She'd dismissed them as the usual things that
happen to children. She'd certainly had her fair
share of bumps and bruises. But Mei Yuk had
never said a word.

Emily fought back the urge to cry. "But Mei
Yuk!" she pleaded. "You love school! Please don't
quit now. You've worked so hard and learned so
much."

"No," Mei Yuk insisted, wiping her eyes with
the back of her hand. "No school. Sorry."

In her heart, Emily couldn't blame her.
How could she encourage Mei Yuk to keep
coming, knowing what she had to endure? At
least there were only two weeks left before the
holidays.

"I'll help you in the summer," she said. "And
maybe in September . . ."

"Maybe." Mei Yuk gave her a small smile. Then
she and Bak Cheun turned and walked away.

It was recess by the time Emily arrived at school.

"Why are you so late?" Alice asked.

Emily told her.

"Tom's a pig!" Alice said with disgust. "I hate him." She paused for a moment, and her expression brightened a bit. "So Mei Yuk isn't coming back to school?"

"You needn't sound so pleased," said Emily.

"I'm not. Not about that."

"What, then?"

"Well . . . now we can be friends again."

Exasperated with Alice and still upset by the morning's events, Emily threw up her hands and cried, "What do you mean, now? Nothing's changed! Mei Yuk is still my friend."

"But that's not fair to me!" Alice wailed. "It's not my fault you made friends with a Chinese girl."

"It's nobody's fault—" Emily was about to say more, but the ringing of the bell put an end to their discussion.

Once in the classroom, she gave Miss Wilson the note her mother had written, explaining Emily's lateness and Mei Yuk's absence.

"I'm sorry," her teacher said. "Do you think she might change her mind and come back?"

Emily shook her head sadly.

A few of her classmates asked about Mei Yuk, but she knew it was more out of curiosity than any real concern. She felt somewhat better when Miss Wilson gave her a primer to take to Mei Yuk, so she could keep up with her lessons. Beyond that, she could only hope that things would be better in the fall.

CHAPTER N° 10

"*Today I'd like you to draw whatever you* please," Miss Carr said as she handed out sheets of paper. "Draw what you did this morning or last Sunday. Draw something you saw on your way to school. Or draw a nursery rhyme."

Emily and the others exchanged glances. So many choices! They never had to make choices like this in school.

"Help yourself to bread," Miss Carr continued. "You know what to do. And no nibbling!" She cast a stern look at her pupils, then turned and busied herself at her easel.

The pupils seized their chance and reached for the bread. Emily took a bite and almost choked. Some of the others coughed and gagged.

"It's full of salt!" Emily shrieked. "Miss Carr! You did it on purpose!"

Miss Carr's shoulders were shaking with laughter, and when she turned around she had a smug look on her face. "I can't have you eating all the erasers, can I? Now, on with your drawings."

"I think I'll draw a nursery rhyme," said Jane. "But, Miss Carr, which one should it be?"

"Whatever takes your fancy. 'Humpty-Dumpty.' 'Jack Be Nimble.' 'London Bridge Is Falling Down.' And don't worry if it doesn't look perfect. Be free and fantastical. Let your imagination soar."

Emily decided to draw "London Bridge." But it wasn't long before she realized that she wasn't drawing the bridge from her picture book. Instead she was drawing Point Ellice Bridge. The centre span had collapsed, and the streetcar was lying at the bottom of the Gorge. People were trapped inside.

Her heart thudded painfully. The nightmare was coming out on the page. She tightened her grip on the charcoal, afraid to continue but unable to stop. She now found herself drawing Florence and the other girl, the one being dragged to the bottom.

This is me . . . Her breath came in ragged gasps. The wide-open eyes. The mouth, a large O. A silent scream . . .

She flung down the charcoal and buried her face in her hands. The room was unusually quiet. Had she screamed out loud?

She felt a hand on her shoulder. "Were you there, Emily Too?" Miss Carr asked gently.

Emily nodded, struggling to hold back the tears. "I have this nightmare . . ."

"And now you've captured it on paper. That's a good place for it, don't you think?" Miss Carr gave her an encouraging smile. "Maybe it won't bother you again."

Emily had never thought of that. If the nightmare were on the page and not in her head . . .

An idea came to her. "I can change it," she said. She erased the two girls and started again. This time, the Emily in the picture was holding Florence's hand and pulling her up to the surface. Emily put smiles on their faces. And then, to make the picture complete, she added Alice.

When she got home, Emily looked at the Door Guardians and came up with another idea. She folded her drawing and tucked it under her pillow, hoping that the true picture would scare away the images in her nightmare. This, after all, was how things had turned out. Emily, Florence, and Alice—all three of them, safe and sound.

On fine days, Miss Carr held her classes outdoors. Accompanied by Watch, the retriever, the whole group set off for the park or the beach armed with easels, folding camp stools, paper, and watercolour boxes.

They could draw or paint whatever they liked—wildflowers, stunted oak trees, the rocky cliffs hugging the sea, or the Olympic Mountains floating in a mist across the strait.

Emily loved these outings. But on this particular day she was feeling less happy than usual. She missed seeing Mei Yuk at school, and her friendship with Alice was not as close as it had been. The fact that this was the last art class of the season only added to her glumness.

At least they were going to Beacon Hill. When the class reached the hillside, Emily settled in the long grass amid the wildflowers and viewed her surroundings.

Miss Carr set up her easel beside her. "What a splendid day," she said cheerfully.

Emily agreed. The day suddenly seemed much brighter with Miss Carr at her side.

"What will you paint today, Emily Too?" her teacher asked.

"Camas lilies," said Emily. "I love the colour." She was becoming quite adept at using her watercolours, and finding the right mix of purple and blue for the camas would be a challenge.

"That'll keep you out of mischief," Miss Carr quipped.

They painted in silence for a while. Then, to make conversation, Emily asked, "What was your favourite place when you were a little girl?"

"Beacon Hill Park," Miss Carr replied.

"Mine too!" said Emily. "What was your favourite thing to do?"

"You mean besides rolling down the hill? I liked to sit on big wooden fences and watch the birds. I liked seeing what the birds were doing."

"I do too!" Emily grinned. They had three things in common! Thinking back to her teacher's earlier remark, she asked, "Did you ever get into mischief?" She immediately wanted to take back the question. Imagine, asking a grown-up that sort of thing! Her mother would be horrified if she knew.

But Miss Carr only laughed. "Oh, yes! One day I took a sick-looking hen into somebody's parlour and doctored it with castor oil. It recovered right on the spot, all over the carpet. And I used to serenade the cow at the top of my lungs. My sisters said the neighbours complained, but I didn't care. I'm still that way, you know. I don't give a hoot what other people think."

Right then and there, Emily decided that she wouldn't give a hoot either. Starting with Alice. She wouldn't worry about their friendship anymore. She just wouldn't care.

CHAPTER N⁰ 11

By the middle of June, Victoria was blossoming with signs of the Diamond Jubilee. Streets, buildings, carriages—the entire city was bedecked with flags and bunting, floral displays, crowns of evergreens, and, above all, pictures of Queen Victoria. Stores had already sold out of the coveted Jubilee brooches, and anyone wanting to buy red, white, or blue cotton was out of luck.

The schools joined in the decorating frenzy, and South Park was no exception. Seated in the Assembly Hall for the year-end awards ceremony,

Emily proudly took in her school's contribution—a huge portrait of Her Majesty surrounded by evergreen boughs and flanked with Canadian ensigns and Union Jacks.

In spite of the festive occasion, she wished that the afternoon would end. Pupils in each class were receiving prizes for attendance, punctuality, deportment, diligence, arithmetic, geography, spelling, writing . . . on and on it went. Emily yawned. She'd won ribbons for races, but she'd never won a prize for schoolwork. Nor did she expect to. Bored and discouraged, she began to count the flags.

A burst of applause drew her attention back to the ceremony. Another diligent pupil . . .

That was the prize Mei Yuk deserved. A prize for diligence and perseverance. Emily knew that Miss Wilson felt the same way. Only that morning her teacher had spoken about Mei Yuk and praised her attitude. She had even told the class they could all take a page out of Mei Yuk's book.

At the front of the hall, Miss Cameron was speaking at the podium. "This year, for the first time, we have a new prize. A book—awarded to the most altruistic pupil in each class."

Altruistic? Emily frowned. What did that mean?

"The books were given by an anonymous friend," Miss Cameron continued. "Someone who wishes to recognize the spirit that prompts one to stop the race for his own advancement, in order to give another a helping hand. Our first winner, in the Fifth Division . . ."

Emily's attention went back to the flags.

"Now we come to the Fourth Division," Miss Cameron was saying. "And the winner is . . . Emily Murdoch!"

At first Emily thought she was hearing things. But when Miss Wilson smiled and said, "Go on! Up you go!" she realized that it was true.

She rose shakily, her face burning with a mixture of excitement and nervousness. The platform seemed so far away. Please don't let me trip, she prayed. Not in front of the whole school!

When she reached the platform, Miss Cameron shook her hand and presented her with her prize. "In two days we celebrate Queen Victoria's Diamond Jubilee," she said. "I can think of no better way to honour Her Majesty than to recognize those who have embraced the feeling of brother-hood and altruism to an outstanding degree. Con-gratulations, Emily. Your prize is well deserved."

"Miss Cameron was wrong. I *don't* deserve it," Emily said at supper that night. "I helped Mei Yuk with her English, but it wasn't enough. All those times, when she was coming to school and getting bullied—I didn't help her with that. And then she gave up."

"You did your best," Mother said. "There are some battles that are too big for one little girl to take on . . . even if she is very brave and determined."

"And artistic," said Amelia.

"You mean *altruistic,*" Jane said. "Isn't that right, Em?"

Emily nodded. "I looked it up. It means being unselfish and considering the welfare of others. I just wish . . ."

"We're proud of you," Father said. "You made a start, and Mei Yuk did, too. That's what's important."

"I'll share my book with her," said Emily. "She can still come here in the summer, can't she?"

"Of course," Mother said. "Mei Yuk will always be welcome here."

On the day of the Jubilee, Emily and her family joined thousands of others on Beacon Hill to take part in an open-air service of thanksgiving. Everyone was dressed up to display their patriotism. White frocks with red and blue sashes, Jubilee brooches, Union Jack neckties, and tricolour hatbands were the order of the day.

The area surrounding the hill had been transformed. Off to the side, a tent city had been set up for visiting soldiers. And at the base of the hill, directly below where Emily and her family were sitting, a pulpit had been erected.

"It's a church with a blue-sky roof," Emily remarked. There would be no rolling down the hill today.

Soon the parade came into view. A grand marshal on a spirited white horse led the way, followed by societies of Englishmen, Irishmen, Scotsmen, native-born Canadians, and pioneers. They marched proudly into the square surrounding the pulpit.

Emily recognized Mr. Kerr among the Sons of Englishmen. She wished that he'd trip and disgrace himself. It would serve him right. Then she remembered that she was in church, in a way, and immediately asked God to forgive her uncharitable thoughts.

Once the marchers and special guests had been seated, the service began. The band played the opening hymn, "All People that on Earth do Dwell," and thousands of voices joined in song. Emily sang out the hymn, hoping that Mr. Kerr and Tom and everyone else would take the words to heart. The hymn meant *all* people. Not just white people.

She thought about this during the sermon and wondered why things had to be so difficult. Getting older didn't seem to change anything. Grown-up Mr. Kerr had the same mean attitude as Tom. He likely encouraged Tom to treat the Chinese badly.

The shrill cry of a bugle interrupted her thoughts and turned her attention to the flagstaff crowning Beacon Hill. As the Royal Standard was hoisted to the top, the band struck up and people raised their voices in the singing of "God Save the Queen."

At the end of the anthem, another minister took his place at the podium. *Another* sermon. Emily groaned silently and tried not to fidget.

"With profound reverence," he began, "do we in this part of the great British Empire join in the thanks which circle the globe today, the sixtieth anniversary of our beloved Queen's reign. Only those who lived before her reign can fully realize the contrast between what was and what is, from merciless oppression and greed to education for the poor and care for the afflicted. These are but some of the precious jewels which by the grace of God adorn Victoria's crown . . ."

Emily's attention wavered. She scanned the crowd, searching for familiar faces, and spotted a woman in a black dress completely covered with little Union Jacks. It turned out to be Mrs. Kerr, and Alice was sitting beside her.

Emily hadn't seen Alice since the end of school. She willed her friend to turn around so she could wave or smile, but Alice seemed intent on listening to the sermon.

Seeing Alice made Emily wonder if she, too, would be attending the military review in Esquimalt the next day. Emily was dreading it. For the first time since the disaster, she would have to go across the Point Ellice Bridge. Her nightmares had miraculously stopped since she'd drawn the picture and placed it under her pillow, but the fear of crossing the bridge remained.

"Look, Em," Amelia whispered beside her. "I'm blowing up my balloon."

"Amelia!" Emily was horrified. She hoped her parents hadn't noticed. People had brought balloons to the service, but you didn't blow them up during the sermon.

The balloon was getting bigger and Amelia was almost out of breath. "Let me tie it," said Emily. She did so, and was about to hand it back when she saw Alice glancing her way. Momentarily distracted, she let go of the balloon.

At the same time, the minister concluded his sermon. Noting this, and seeing the balloon

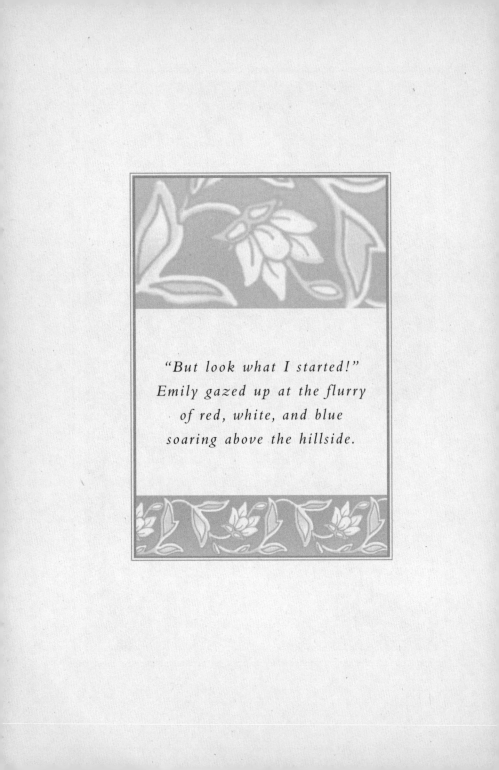

"But look what I started!"
Emily gazed up at the flurry
of red, white, and blue
soaring above the hillside.

floating overhead, many people took it as a signal to release theirs.

"You lost my balloon!" Amelia sniffed.

"But look what I started!" Emily gazed up at the flurry of red, white, and blue soaring above the hillside. It was almost like an offering. She sent a prayer along with it—that tomorrow she would safely cross over the bridge.

"I can do it, I can do it . . ." Emily chanted the words as she took a seat in the crowded streetcar. She'd insisted on sitting on the right-hand side, as if it would once again be lucky. She also insisted that Father open the window.

She remained calm during the ride through town, but as the streetcar rolled onto the bridge she clenched her fists and squeezed her eyes shut. "I can do it . . ."

Father tried to reassure her by saying that lightning never struck the same spot twice. But Emily knew it wasn't true. Three years before the disaster, on the same 24th of May holiday, the same bridge had sagged under the weight of the very same car. It was only luck that had saved the passengers that day. Would today be a lucky day?

"Don't worry, dear," Mother said. "It's a brand-new bridge. It's built to carry heavy loads."

"I know," said Emily, "but I can't help thinking . . ."

Were they almost across? She risked a peek. Directly below, the waters of the Gorge glinted in the sunlight. She covered her eyes as a knot of fear rose up in her throat. She felt trapped inside her nightmare, unable to breathe. If only she'd thought to bring her drawing . . .

But she could draw it in her mind. Three girls smiling on the surface of the water. That was the truth. Her nightmare was only a might-have-been.

The clanging of the bell made her risk another peek. "We're back on land!" she exclaimed. "We really made it across?"

"Indeed we did," Father said.

"We still have to go back," she said anxiously.

"Yes, but let's cross that bridge when we come to it. All right? Put it out of your mind and enjoy the day."

Emily promised to try.

The grounds were packed by the time they reached Macaulay Point, but Father managed to find a spot that afforded a good view of the troops.

"When does the *jam battle* start?" Amelia asked.

"It's *sham* battle," Emily said. "Don't you remember? And there isn't a battle this time. It's only a review."

"There's marching and big guns going off," said Jane.

"Big guns?"

"Yes, but they're fired into the air and nobody gets hurt."

"Except when little girls ask too many questions," Emily said. "Then they bring out the cannons—" She broke off, leaving the sentence unfinished. "There's Alice!"

Alice was standing with her mother a short distance away. She must have come across the bridge too. Had it been as difficult for her? Emily felt a welling up inside. In spite of her determination not to give a hoot, as Miss Carr put it, she couldn't help but care. She and Alice had gone through the same terrifying experience and shared a bond too powerful to break. She had to smooth things over.

She thought for a moment and came up with an idea. After a few words to her parents, she picked her way through the crowd to talk to Alice.

Alice smiled when she saw her. "Hello, Emily," she said. "Congratulations on your prize. You deserved it."

"Thank you," Emily said. Then, "Alice, I was wondering . . ." She glanced nervously at Mrs. Kerr, took a deep breath, and plunged ahead.

"Would you like to come to the Illuminations with us tonight?"

Alice's face lit up. "May I?" she asked her mother.

Before Mrs. Kerr could reply, Emily added, "Mei Yuk's coming, too."

Mrs. Kerr bristled. "I'm surprised that you would ask, Emily."

"I asked because it's a special celebration and I want to share it. Alice is my best friend. But Mei Yuk is my friend, too, and I won't choose between them." She turned to Alice. "I wanted you to know that. I guess the rest is up to you."

As Alice was about to speak, a firing of guns signalled the start of the review.

"I'd better go back to my parents," Emily said. "Goodbye, Alice."

She hadn't gone far when Alice caught up. "Here," she said. She removed her Jubilee brooch and pressed it into Emily's hand. "Give this to Mei Yuk and tell her I'm sorry. Maybe one day . . ."

"I hope so," Emily said, and gave her a hug.

CHAPTER N⁰ 12

"Fire!" Mei Yuk exclaimed. Her face shone in the night.

Emily nodded excitedly.

They were standing on the summit of Beacon Hill and the enormous beacon fires had just been set ablaze. A fiery chain encircled the city, from Race Rocks in the west to Oak Bay in the east. And that wasn't all. Rockets and Roman candles were exploding in the sky, in showers of red, white, and blue.

"Will they see us from across the strait?" Emily wondered. The American side looked so close.

"They'll certainly see the beacons," her father said. "And to think that this is happening in every dominion that flies the British flag."

"The whole world is lit up," said Emily.

"Not the *whole* world," Jane argued.

"Well, almost. Miss Wilson told us that Queen Victoria rules 11 million square miles of land and 400 million people."

"How does she do that?" asked Amelia.

Emily shrugged. "I guess queens just know about that sort of thing."

After the fireworks display was over, they set off for the Inner Harbour to see the Illuminations, centred around the newly completed parliament buildings.

Emily held her breath in awe. She had often walked past the new parliament buildings but had never seen them like this. The entire design was traced with lights, from the basement to the tip of the dome. Lights streamed from every window. Above the main entrance, a royal crown glowed in coloured fire. On top of the dome, the gold statue of Captain Vancouver glittered with light, and the torch in his hand shone like a star.

Mei Yuk gasped in wonder.

"It's a fairyland," Emily sighed. "It's like magic."

"Magic," Mei Yuk repeated, savouring the word. "Magic."

Emily gazed at the lights, spellbound. She couldn't help but remember the Illuminations held during the previous year—the parade of boats trailing along the Gorge Waterway, people standing on the Point Ellice Bridge singing "God Save the Queen" . . . How happy she'd been that night. Yet within twenty-four hours, disaster had struck.

What would the next twenty-four hours bring? The next month? The next year?

One thing was certain. The memory of the disaster no longer filled her with dread. She had crossed over the bridge, twice in one day. It was bound to be easier the next time.

As for her friendship with Alice, it was up to Alice to make the next move. And whatever

Alice decided . . . Emily gave a determined smile and said to herself, I'll just cross that bridge when I come to it.

Acknowledgements

Thanks to Kerry Mason, art historian and consultant, and to Kathryn Bridge, manager of Access Services, B.C. Archives, for reading the sections on Emily Carr and checking for accuracy. And an enormous thank you to my friend Charlayne Thornton-Joe for her valuable comments, her encouragement, and her tireless commitment to "building bridges."

Dear Reader,

Welcome back to the continuing adventures of Our Canadian Girl! It's been another exciting year for the series, with ten girls' stories published and two more on the way! In January you'll meet Keeley, who moves to the newly established town of Frank, Alberta, in 1901, and Millie, a Toronto girl spending the summer of 1914 in the Kawarthas.

So please keep on reading. And do stay in touch. Write to us, log on to our website. We love to hear from you!

Sincerely,
Barbara Berson
Editor

Canada's

1608
Samuel de
Champlain
establishes
the first
fortified
trading post
at Quebec.

1759
The British
defeat the
French in
the Battle
of the
Plains of
Abraham.

1812
The United
States
declares war
against
Canada.

1845
The expedition of
Sir John Franklin
to the Arctic ends
when the ship is
frozen in the pack
ice; the fate of its
crew remains a
mystery.

1869
Louis Riel
leads his
Métis
followers in
the Red
River
Rebellion.

1871
British
Columbia
joins
Canada.

1755
The British
expel the
entire French
population
of Acadia
(today's
Maritime
provinces),
sending
them into
exile.

1776
The 13
Colonies
revolt
against
Britain, and
the Loyalists
flee to
Canada.

1837
Calling for
responsible
government, the
Patriotes, following
Louis-Joseph
Papineau, rebel in
Lower Canada;
William Lyon
Mackenzie leads the
uprising in Upper
Canada.

1867
New
Brunswick,
Nova Scotia,
and the United
Province of
Canada come
together in
Confederation
to form the
Dominion of
Canada.

1870
Manitoba joins
Canada. The
Northwest
Territories
becomes an
official
territory of
Canada.

1784
Rachel

Timeline

1885
At Craigellachie, British Columbia, the last spike is driven to complete the building of the Canadian Pacific Railway.

1898
The Yukon Territory becomes an official territory of Canada.

1914
Britain declares war on Germany, and Canada, because of its ties to Britain, is at war too.

1918
As a result of the Wartime Elections Act, the women of Canada are given the right to vote in federal elections.

1945
World War II ends conclusively with the dropping of atomic bombs on Hiroshima and Nagasaki.

1873
Prince Edward Island joins Canada.

1896
Gold is discovered on Bonanza Creek, a tributary of the Klondike River.

1905
Alberta and Saskatchewan join Canada.

1917
In the Halifax harbour, two ships collide, causing an explosion that leaves more than 1,600 dead and 9,000 injured.

1939
Canada declares war on Germany seven days after war is declared by Britain and France.

1949
Newfoundland, under the leadership of Joey Smallwood, joins Canada.

1885
Marie-Claire

1897
Emily

1918
Penelope

Check out the
Our Canadian Girl website

Fun Stuff

- E-cards
- Prizes
- Activities
- Poll

Fan Area

- Guest Book
- Photo Gallery
- Downloadable *Our Canadian Girl* Tea Party Kit

Features on the girls and more!

www.ourcanadiangirl.ca